KIDNAPPED

by R. L. Stevenson
Retold as a play by Keith West

Illustrations by William Boucher,
taken from the serialised version of *Kidnapped*, 1886

About this play

This play is a dramatised version of the novel *Kidnapped* by Robert Louis Stevenson which was first published in 1886. The illustrations used in this play are taken from the first edition of the novel.

Robert Louis Stevenson (1850 – 1894) is regarded as one of the greatest adventure writers of all time. Stevenson believed that 'no man was any use until he had dared everything.' He made sure that his own life was packed with incident and adventure, which is remarkable considering he suffered from poor health all of his life. He was born in Edinburgh, Scotland – but visited America, the South Seas and Samoa. It was the city of Edinburgh that gave Stevenson some of his ideas for Kidnapped.

The book is set after the battle of Culloden Moor, which is a place near Inverness. Bonnie Prince Charlie believed he was the rightful king of Britain as he was a descendant of the Stuart kings. Instead of a Stuart king, Britain was ruled by the son of a German-speaker, King George II. Bonnie Prince Charlie was leader of the Jacobites – the Jacobites wanted the Bonnie Prince to replace King George II.

Earlier, in 1715, James Edward Stuart had raised a rebellion against England. The rebellion failed. The Bonnie Prince led the Jacobite rebellion in 1746. The Jacobites were heavily defeated and he had to flee for his life. In fact, Prince Charles was forced to remain in exile until his death, but his supporters always hoped he would return with an army and defeat the English.

The English forces blamed the Highlanders for the rebellion and treated them very badly. The Lowlanders generally sided with the English, and so they were hated by the Highlanders.

In this play, I have taken some liberties by adding an extra scene, bringing in the Battle of Culloden. In the original script, Alan the adventurer had fought on both the side of the King and with the Jacobite rebels – doing whatever suited him best. However, I have made him most definitely a Highlander.

I hope that my adaptation of the novel carries some of the adventurous spirit of the original, and encourages a new generation to read the full story.

Keith West 2000

CHARACTERS

David Balfour	as an old man
David Balfour	as a seventeen-year-old
Alexander Balfour	David's father
Doctor Donald	Alexander's doctor
Merchant	
Barber	
Old woman	known as Jennet Clouston
Ebenezer Balfour	David's uncle
Mr Campbell	Minister of Essendean
The Sailor	
Captain Hoseason	Captain of the brig 'Covenant'
Mr Riach	Captain Hoseason's righthand man
Alan Breck	alias Mr Thompson
Sailors/soldiers	(Mostly non-speaking)
Duncan McKiegh	Blind man. A Highlander
Neil Roy	A Highlander
Colin Roy Campbell	King George's friend
Mungo	Colin Roy's friend
Cluny Macpherson	A Highlander
Mr Rankeillor	Lawyer
James Stewart	related to royalty (Stuarts)
Ardshiel	Leader of the clans
Old Man	A Highlander

Dedicated to the late David J. Lyon,
who fostered my love of literature.

ACT ONE   SCENE ONE

The battle of Culloden, 1746. The Highlanders have lost and King George's men are killing as many of the enemy as they can. It is the end of the Jacobite uprising. Alan Breck, Neil Roy and other Jacobites are talking, during the battle.

ALAN: This is a bad day for Bonnie Prince Charlie and our Highland forces.

NEIL: We are being massacred.

ALAN: We will never recover. King George II of England will make paupers of us because of this rebellion.

NEIL: We need to hide Bonnie Prince Charles, or they will hang him.

ALAN: He has to go to France. The French will look after him until the time is right.

ARDSHIEL: I'll go with him. Time to flee from the battlefield, Alan.

(Later, the rebels are in hiding near Inverness)

JAMES: Bonnie Prince Charlie is my kinsman. *(Laughs)* I hold the family name, James Stewart. Little good has that name ever done anyone. *(Afraid)* What if we're caught?

CLUNY: Pull yourself together, man. Caught? No! I'll hide in the caves east of here. There are so many underground passages. I could hide an army for a thousand years. Any injuries?

NEIL:	*(Sadly)* Many of our dear friends are dead, and Duncan McKiegh is blinded.
ALAN:	*(Taking charge)* This is a black day indeed – but it is essential we take the Bonnie Prince to France. I'll hide with him.
ARDSHIEL:	I'll come with you, as leader of the clan.
NEIL:	And I'll take Duncan to his home in Mull. May we meet again!
ALAN:	And until we do meet once more -

NEIL:	}	
CLUNY:	}	A curse on King George and the traitor
JAMES:	}	Campbell Clan!
ARDSHIEL:	}	

SCENE TWO

David Balfour, as an old man, is narrating his story. He is talking about his adventures in 1751, five years after the failed Jacobite uprising when he was a young boy of seventeen.

OLD DAVID:	*(Narrating)* My parents died suddenly. My mother had a severe fever and passed away. As soon as she died, my father took ill. Before he died, he asked to see me. He was sitting in bed. The doctor and I were attending him.
ALEXANDER:	*(To young David)* Davie, my boy, I want you to take a letter from the top of my drawer. That letter is your inheritance.
DAVID:	I'll fetch the letter, father. Don't worry, just rest.

5

ALEXANDER:	*(Struggling to sit up)* I have a brother, Davie. He's a mean man, a mean man indeed. But he has his reasons.
DOCTOR:	*(To Alexander)* Do not talk, Alex. Your boy is right, you need your rest.
ALEXANDER:	*(To Doctor)* Oh, Donald … you know I am as good as dead. *(Coughs)* You know I don't have long.
DAVID:	*(Holds the letter)* Is this the letter for my uncle?
ALEXANDER:	Uncle Ebenezer. Yes indeed. *(Coughs)* And my soul cries out that I am doing you wrong, Davie. I am wrong to send you to the house of Shaws, my family home.
DOCTOR:	*(Alarmed)* Alexander - you must rest!
ALEXANDER:	*(Sadly)* I shall rest enough when I've joined my dear wife.
DAVID:	*(Kindly)* You need to fight this illness, father. You may yet live.
ALEXANDER:	*(Coughing)* I ran away from the house of Shaws when I was about your age, Davie. But I'm afraid you must return.
DAVID:	*(Kindly)* Don't you worry about anything, father.
ALEXANDER:	Worry? But you have to return to that accursed place. And Ebenezer, *(cough)* he's not like me, Davie, not like me at all!
DOCTOR:	Rest yourself, Alexander. Most of all you need rest.

ALEXANDER: *(Coughs)* Aye!

DAVID: *(Alarmed)* Doctor!

(Alexander Balfour falls back on the bed)

DOCTOR: *(Examining Alexander)* Davie, lad, I am afraid your good father has joined your dear mother. He is dead!

SCENE THREE

David is about to depart for the house of Shaws.

OLD DAVID: *(Narrating)* After my father's burial, I knew I had to travel to the house of Shaws, near Edinburgh. This meant a two-day walk for a young and fit boy – such as I was in those days. Before I left my home in Essendean, Mr Campbell, the minister, came to say farewell.

MR CAMPBELL: Are you sorry to leave Essendean, Davie?

DAVID: I'm not sure. I've never lived anywhere else.

MR CAMPBELL: I have seen the letter that your father called your inheritance. This letter should be your admittance into that grand house.

DAVID: *(Reading the letter again)* To the hands of Ebenezer Balfour, esquire, of Shaws – this will be delivered by my son, David Balfour.

MR CAMPBELL: Your father was related to the Shaws in some way. Your uncle still lives in the family home. Although your father was a poor schoolmaster here, in Essendean, I always thought he came from gentle stock.

DAVID: I'm seventeen years old, and neither of my parents told me anything about my ancestors.

MR CAMPBELL: You may have high relations, but you were brought up in the country, as your mother and father felt it right to do.

DAVID: What would you do in my shoes, Mr Campbell? Would you go to the house of Shaws?

MR CAMPBELL: Why yes! What have you got to lose? A two-day walk there – and if your high relations don't want you, you can walk back here. I see no danger for you!

SCENE FOUR

On his way to Edinburgh, David asks several people if they know the way to the house of Shaws. He always receives odd reactions. He begins to feel there is something strange about the house of Shaws. Eventually, he asks a merchant who is driving his cart.

DAVID: Do you know the house of Shaws?

MERCHANT: Aye – I know it.

DAVID: It's a great house, I suppose.

MERCHANT: Doubtless. The house is a grand big place.

DAVID: Who lives in the house? Grand folk? Friendly folk?

MERCHANT: Folk? Are you daft? Nobody lives there that you'd call friendly folk.

DAVID: And does Mr Ebenezer Balfour live there?

MERCHANT: Oh aye. The Laird lives there. What do you want with the Laird?

DAVID: Perhaps he'll find me a job.

MERCHANT: *(Incredulous)* What? A job? *(He peers down from his cart)* You seem a decent sort of boy. If you'll take my advice, you'll keep clear of the place!

(David walks on until he meets a barber in a small town – he thinks barbers will know all the gossip)

DAVID: What kind of a man is Ebenezer Balfour?

BARBER: Ha, ha, ha. He's not a good kind of a man at all.

(David walks on until he meets an old woman)

OLD WOMAN: Look down the valley. Look at that great bulk of a building. That is the house of Shaws.

DAVID: That? But it looks like a ruin.

OLD WOMAN: *(Becoming agitated)* That is the house of Shaws! Blood built it; blood stopped the building of it; blood shall bring it down. *(She spits on the ground)* Soon may the place fall down! If you meet the Laird, old Ebenezer, tell him all you hear. I'm Jennet Clouston and I have cursed his house twelve hundred and nineteen times. Barn, stable, man, guest, and master, wife, miss or child – may destruction come upon them all!

DAVID: But....*(he sees her hurrying away)*...like a witch she is gone!

(David walks towards the house of Shaws)

9

OLD DAVID:	*(Narrating)* I crept courteously up to the door of the house and knocked. I was scared. All I wanted to do was turn and walk back to Essendean. Then I heard a cough above me. In a first-storey window was an old man in a nightcap. He held a blunderbuss in his hands.
EBENEZER:	It's loaded.
DAVID:	*(Shouts up)* I have a letter – for Mr Ebenezer Balfour.
EBENEZER:	From whom?
DAVID:	I shan't tell you until you let me into your house.
EBENEZER:	You can put the letter on the doorstep – and be off!
DAVID:	But it's a letter of introduction. I must see Mr Ebenezer Balfour.
EBENEZER:	Who are you?
DAVID:	I am David Balfour.
EBENEZER:	*(Quietly)* Is your father dead? *(Silence)* Ay, he'll be dead alright, that's what brings his son to the house of Shaws. *(To David)* Wait, and I'll let you in! I'm your uncle, I'll have to let you in!
	(In a short while there comes a great rattling of chains and bolts. The door is opened cautiously. As soon as David creeps into the house, it is locked and barred behind him. Ebenezer speaks without ever looking David in the eye)
	Go into the kitchen and touch nothing.
	(The kitchen is almost empty, except for a bright

*fire and half a dozen dishes stacked on a shelf.
The table is laid for supper with a bowl of
porridge, a wooden spoon and a cup of beer)*

DAVID: This is the barest room I have ever seen!

EBENEZER: Aye, so it is!

*(David notices that Ebenezer is narrow-
shouldered and stooping. His face is grey. He
wears a flannel nightgown over a ragged shirt,
and a flannel nightcap.)*

DAVID: *(Surprised)* Father always wore a coat and
waistcoat.

EBENEZER: Aye – most men do.

DAVID: You're unshaven! Are you Mr Ebenezer?

EBENEZER: I am Mr Ebenezer. Are you hungry? Could
you do with some porridge?

DAVID: I cannot eat your supper.

EBENEZER:	I'll take the ale, it'll help my cough. So Alexander's dead?
	(David nods)
	You're my nephew?
	(David nods)
	If you can't eat the porridge, I'll take it.
DAVID:	*(Not liking Ebenezer)* I've lost my appetite!
EBENEZER:	Your father never liked a great deal of food. Alexander been long dead?
DAVID:	Three weeks, sir.
EBENEZER:	He was a secret man. Has he ever spoken of me?
DAVID:	No – never, except – when he was dying.
EBENEZER:	A strange man, your father. *(Pause)* I'm glad I let you in. We'll get along fine! I'll show you to your bed. We have no lights here. I'm frightened of candles. They cause fires! Your bed may be a wee bit damp, Davie.

SCENE FIVE

The following day, David is talking to his uncle over a bowl of breakfast porridge

EBENEZER:	You can stay here, Davie – you must write to nobody.
DAVID:	But - I promised Mr Campbell.

EBENEZER:	In a day or two, I'll set you up in a job. What would you like – the army?
DAVID:	Well…
EBENEZER:	The ministry?
DAVID:	I…
EBENEZER:	Law! I'll set you up in Law. We Balfours are a proud race. The Law it is! You'll do fine by me. What's mine is yours, Davie and what's yours is mine.
DAVID:	Last night, I thought you were a miser.
EBENEZER:	Miser? Why no – I am a generous man. Now I have to venture out, alone. Business! I cannot let you have this place to yourself, though. I must lock you outside, until I return.
DAVID:	*(Shocked)* Uncle!
EBENEZER:	Aye, well, you cannot stay inside.
DAVID:	Do you think I am a common thief?
EBENEZER:	Well, well! I'll not go out.
DAVID:	If you don't trust me, I'll go back home to Essendean. Mr Campbell will look after me.
EBENEZER:	*(Laughs)* No, no, no. I like you fine. You stay here and I shall stay with you. We'll get to know each other better, much better! *(Suddenly)* I promised your father I'd give you forty pounds, if he died first. Now hide yourself while I search for the money. Nobody can say my word is not my bond.

DAVID: *(To himself)* I wish my uncle would look me in the eye. He appears so shifty!

EBENEZER: *(Counting out his money)* I'm growing old – here's your forty pounds – but you must help me with the housework and garden. I'm a little broken down!

DAVID: I'll help you as much as I can.

EBENEZER: *(Brightening)* Good, glad to hear it! *(He produces a key)* Now go up the steps of the stair tower and fetch me my papers. That part of the house is not finished, so take care.

DAVID: Can I have a light, to help me up the stairs?

EBENEZER: *(Slyly)* No – we don't have lights in the house.

DAVID: Are the stairs good?

EBENEZER: They're grand – but there are no banisters. Keep to the wall and you'll do fine! Remember, the house is five storeys high.

OLD DAVID: *(Narrating)* My uncle intended to kill me. I was saved by a flash of lightning that revealed the stairs had never been completed. If I had climbed to the top, I would have fallen to my death. I sneaked back to the kitchen, where my uncle sat. I placed my arms upon his shoulders.

DAVID: Ah!

(Uncle Ebenezer faints)

Uncle! What is the matter? Did you think I was a ghost?

EBENEZER: Davie boy, the blue phial…in the cupboard…my heart is not so good.

DAVID: Uncle, why did you try to kill me?

EBENEZER: I'll tell you in the morning. My heart! Go to sleep!

SCENE SIX

DAVID: *(To himself)* I think my uncle hates me. I'm sure I'm in danger. *(laughs)* They say the Warlock of Essendean has a mirror in which man can read the future. I could do with the mirror now. Or perhaps not!

EBENEZER: *(Shouting upstairs)* Davie, your porridge is ready!

DAVID: *(To himself)* Does my uncle ever eat anything but porridge? *(Walking downstairs)* Perhaps my uncle will tell me the truth. Why did he want me dead?

(David enters the kitchen)

EBENEZER: Sit down, laddie, and eat your porridge.

DAVID: What cause have you to fear me, to cheat me and to try to kill…

EBENEZER: *(Laughs)* Oh, a mere jest, Davie. I thought you'd have the humour of your father!

(There is a knocking on the door)

DAVID: Don't stir yourself, Uncle.

(David opens the door. A sailor stands there. He is grinning)

SAILOR: Whatcha, mate! I've a letter for Mr Balfour and I'm mortal hungry.

DAVID: Well, come into the house.

(Uncle Ebenezer reads the letter)

EBENEZER: Ah, it's from Captain Hoseason. He has a trading brig, the 'Covenant'. I must go and see him. Are you coming with me, David lad?

DAVID: Being a country boy, I've hardly ever seen the sea.

EBENEZER: Good. Very well! Come with me!

(The threesome walk to the seaside. David is shown the 'Covenant', which is getting ready to sail)

EBENEZER: *(Spotting the Captain)* Ah, Hoseason. I have some business in the town. *(He winks at the Captain)* Will you entertain my nephew, David, for a short while?

CAPTAIN: Why, yes, of course. Ever seen round a ship, David?

DAVID: No, I can't say that I have.

CAPTAIN: We need to row out to her; and I'll show you around.

EBENEZER: Be back before noon. *(He winks again)*

CAPTAIN: Aye, aye, sir!

(Later, after David is shown around)

DAVID: But, the ship's moving.

CAPTAIN: Aye, that it is, Davie.

DAVID: But my uncle? *(Sudden dawn of realisation)* I've been kidnapped. Help!

(The sailor hits David over the head, with a large piece of wood. He falls to the floor, in a faint)

SCENE SEVEN

David awakes to voices. He knows two people are talking about him. The wound to his head and the movement of the ship make David feel sick

CAPTAIN:	I am no conjurer, Mr Riach.
RIACH:	I want that boy taken out of this hole and put in the forecastle.
CAPTAIN:	What you may want and what you may have are two different things. Here he is; here he shall stay.
RIACH:	I bet the old man paid you well.
CAPTAIN:	*(Angry)* Keep your breath to cool your porridge.
RIACH:	Were you paid to murder the boy?
CAPTAIN:	No, not murder!
RIACH:	The lad has a fever.
CAPTAIN:	Go drink yourself to death, Riach. The boy stays here!
RIACH:	I'll not go unless the boy is taken upstairs!
	(David swoons again. When he wakes up, he finds himself in a bed in the forecastle)
RIACH:	You alright, laddie?
DAVID:	I think I shall be when the seasickness goes.
RIACH:	Ah well, ready to be a slave in the Americas. You'll be hoeing tobacco overseas soon, if Captain Hoseason and your wicked uncle get their way.
DAVID:	*(Alarmed)* You must help me. I need to write to Mr Campbell of Essendean.

RIACH:	Sorry – I can't do that for you.
	(David is forced to serve as cabin boy. One night there is a thudding crash)
RIACH:	The ship, she's struck!
CAPTAIN:	No sir, no. We've hit a small boat, 'tis all!
RIACH:	*(Looking over the side)* The boat's sinking.
DAVID:	They're all going to die!
CAPTAIN:	All except one. Look, he's caught the brig's bowspit.
RIACH:	That man has unusual strength!
ALAN:	*(Smiling as Mr Riach hauls him aboard)* Ah, you've saved my life!
CAPTAIN:	I don't know why. You've a French coat on your back, even if you've got a Scottish tongue in your head.
ALAN:	I'm a Jacobite – and a true Scot. I had to escape King George's men. I would have been hanged for sure.
CAPTAIN:	You'll be a Jacobite then?
ALAN:	Aye, that I am! I just told you so!
CAPTAIN:	We'll leave you alone then. Eat as much food as you find below deck.
ALAN:	*(Sadly)* My men are all drowned. They were good people. They would have died for me if necessary.

CAPTAIN:	*(Harsh)* I would weep for the boat. Men are two a penny. A boat is expensive and hard to come by.
ALAN:	But *(sad)* they were my friends. Loyalty is not easy to find.
CAPTAIN:	Friends? There are no friends on the open seas. It's every man for himself. Come with me, David.
	(The Captain takes Riach aside)
	Riach, assemble the men. That stranger is rich. His pistols are those of a gentleman. He carries a bag of gold, to be sure.
RIACH:	We can't just murder the man.
CAPTAIN:	He is a Jacobite and a traitor. It is our duty to kill him.
DAVID:	But, murder! No, I can't take part in any murder.
CAPTAIN:	*(Sharp)* David - below decks with you!
	(To Riach) We'll ask the men.
	(David quickly finds the stranger)
DAVID:	Do you want to die?
ALAN:	*(Jumps up from the Captain's table)* No!
DAVID:	The ship's crew plan to murder you for your money.
ALAN:	And who are you?

DAVID:	David Balfour, Sir.
ALAN:	They call me Alan Breck. Now do me a favour and charge my pistols. I'll hold them back with my sword.
DAVID:	We'll both be killed. *(Brightens)* Better dead than a slave! *(Angry)* They plan to sell me when they arrive in the Americas.
ALAN:	How many of the ship's crew will be against us?
DAVID:	Fifteen.
	(Alan whistles)
ALAN:	There's nothing we can do about that. You guard the back door with my pistols. I'll keep them busy with the sword.
DAVID:	But, I'm no great shot!
ALAN:	I'm glad to see you're honest. Just do your best.
	(The Captain tries to enter the door)
ALAN:	*(Sword in hand)* Stand!
CAPTAIN:	A drawn sword? This is a strange return for my hospitality. *(Glances at David)*
ALAN:	I've killed many of King George's men with my sword. You and your crew may attack now – the sooner the battle starts, the better.
CAPTAIN:	*(Glancing at David again)* Davie, I'll make sure you suffer for your treachery. *(The Captain backs away)*

(Later, the crew try to attack)

ALAN: *(Looking at his bloody sword)* Got one of them, David!

(Two men attack and David tries the pistols)

DAVID: *(Shocked but delighted)* I have one!

ALAN: You're a brave lad, David.

RIACH: *(Shouts through the door)* This is a bad job. The Captain wants to speak to you both.

ALAN: I don't trust the Captain.

CAPTAIN: *(Shouting from outside)* I've lost too many men. I'll have to sail for Glasgow and find more sailors. I'll bargain with you. Give me twelve pounds and I'll put you and Davie ashore.

ALAN:	*(Thinking)* I'll have to trust you. *(To David)* He'll starve us out!
CAPTAIN:	*(Opening the door)* You're a good fighting man. I fear for my life. A bargain?
ALAN:	*(Finally)* Done. But if you try treachery, I'll kill you first.

(The Captain departs, hastily)

OLD DAVID:	*(Narrating)* Alan suggested we tell each other our stories over breakfast. I told him all my misfortunes and mentioned I would like to be back with my friend, Mr Campbell. Alan lost his temper.
ALAN:	Campbell? I hate the name. The only help I'd give a Campbell is a bullet in the heart.
DAVID:	*(Puzzled)* Why? Why do you hate the Campbells so much?
ALAN:	Because I'm a Stewart. The Campbells have tried to kill us, they changed the law against us and tricked us out of land and riches. I was so poor, I enlisted into King George's army. But I deserted and joined the Jacobites.
DAVID:	But deserting the King's army and joining the rebels means death.
ALAN:	If they get their hands on me, I'd swing, for sure. I am now commissioned by the French king! Really, I carry money from the Highlanders to give to their exiled leader – Ardshiel. After he lost the battle of Culloden, Ardshiel had to flee the country, or be hanged.

DAVID:	Didn't the English strip him of his lands?
ALAN:	Aye, if a man wears a kilt he'll be put in jail. They took everything – except the love; the Clansmen love their chief. But there is still a problem.
DAVID:	What is that?
ALAN:	King George put a Campbell – Colin Roy – in charge of collecting a rent from us Highlanders. Colin Roy, we call him Red Fox, wants to starve all Stewarts. He has taken all our land, wealth and weapons. If I see him, he will die!

SCENE EIGHT

There is a crashing sound and the brig 'Covenant' lurches wildly.

CAPTAIN:	*(Shouts)* Out, out, or you are doomed. The good brig 'Covenant' is sinking fast.
ALAN:	*(Drawing his sword)* You had better not be tricking us.
CAPTAIN:	No trick! It's everyone for himself. We are near the Island of Mull.
ALAN:	*(To himself)* Mull?
CAPTAIN:	Help us man the lifeboats. You have injured so many of our men. I need extra hands.
DAVID:	We'll help you all we can.
	(There is a sickening crash)

RIACH: Man the small boats, or we drown.

(On deck there is panic. The brig lurches sideways and David is thrown overboard)

OLD DAVID: *(Narrating)* I did not know what happened to Alan Breck – I just hoped my new friend had not drowned. He told me, many weeks later, what had happened.

(Alan and the sailors land from the lifeboat)

CAPTAIN: Men – this is open space and the boy is nowhere to be seen. We'll kill this Jacobite yet. He has no place to hide.

RIACH: No, we cannot kill him, Captain Hoseason. The man has helped us.

CAPTAIN: That Jacobite is alone. He has a great deal of money on him.

ALAN: Liar!

CAPTAIN: *(To his men)* 'The Covenant' is lost, some of your comrades are dead. We need revenge.

ALAN: *(Drawing his sword)* Seven against one – I'm not afraid, I'll fight you all.

RIACH: *(To the men)* No, you cannot kill the Jacobite. If you try, I'll fight with him. From this moment on, I'll have nothing more to do with Captain Hoseason. Run, Alan Breck, run.

ALAN: *(Waving his sword in the air)* Thank you, Mr Riach. From now on, I shall account you a friend.

ACT TWO   SCENE ONE

OLD DAVID: *(Narrating)* I swam to a small island and eventually made my way to Mull. I could not believe that someone like Alan Breck had drowned, and set out to look for him. Eventually I found a very poor old man who was able to help.

DAVID: Old man, have you seen any sailors, recently shipwrecked?

OLD MAN: Aye, laddie, I have.

DAVID: Was there one amongst them dressed like a gentleman?

OLD MAN: *(Standing up)* You must be the laddie that the gentleman asked about.

DAVID: Yes.

OLD MAN: I have a word for you. You are to follow your friend to his country, by Torosay. Duncan McKiegh will guide you. *(Shouts)* Hey, Duncan!

(A blind man tapping with a stick comes up to David)

DAVID: This man is blind, how can he guide me to Torosay?

DUNCAN: I might be blind, but I know every stone, heath and bush on this island. I'll take you to Torosay for a drink of brandy.

DAVID: *(Laughing)* Done! A bargain!

(David notices Duncan has a pistol that he is hiding under his cloak)

DUNCAN: *(Walking fast, tapping his stick)* And where do you come from, eh?

DAVID: Essendean.

DUNCAN: Ah, Campbell country. Are you rich, my boy? Can you change a five-shilling piece for me?

(David keeps swapping sides along the track, so that Duncan cannot shoot him)

DUNCAN: Why are you jumping in and out like a jack-in-a-box?

DAVID: You have a pistol and I fear you might use it. *(Lying)* I have one in my pocket and it's aimed for your heart.

DUNCAN: Oh, have you now! You wouldn't harm a poor, blind man, would you? Now when we arrive at Torosay, you can cross to the mainland. I will introduce you to a friend.

(They reach the port)

DUNCAN:	*(Tasting the drink of brandy)* Neil Roy, this is David Balfour.
NEIL:	Friend of Alan Breck! A friend of Alan's is my friend. I shall give you the route. Speak to no one on the way. Avoid the King's men, the Campbells and red soldiers. Act like a Jacobite and you'll come to no harm from the local people. The people here are starving, thanks to King George. Don't mention the name Alan Breck. There is a price on his life and he has to be careful.
DAVID:	I'll not mention his name.
NEIL:	*(Spitting on the ground)* Colin Campbell is the evil one working for King George, he is forcing tenants out of their homes. People here are starving.
DAVID:	I'll be on my way and I shall try to avoid Colin Campbell.
	(David has only walked a short way when two riders accost him)
COLIN:	I am Colin Roy Campbell, Red Fox. What are you doing out here?
DAVID:	I am on my way to Aucharn.
COLIN:	And what do you seek in Aucharn?
DAVID:	The ... the man that lives there.
COLIN:	*(musing)* James of the Glens.
MUNGO:	Ah, he seeks James Stewart, don't you think, Colin?

COLIN: We cannot trust him, Mungo.

DAVID: I am neither of his people, nor yours. I am an honest subject of King George.

(A gunshot is heard and Colin Roy Campbell falls from his horse)

COLIN: I am dying, I am dying.

(Mungo jumps from his horse and attends the injured man)

MUNGO: You are only wounded, man.

COLIN: Take care – snipers – oh I am dying.

(His head rolls on his shoulders and he is dead)

DAVID: *(Scrambling up the hillside)* Murderers!

(David spots the sniper)

Up here, I see him!

(The redcoats arrive on the scene)

MUNGO: *(To the soldiers)* Ten pound for the lad. Get him, he's an accomplice. He was posted here to hold us in talk, while the sniper shot us!

DAVID: No!

(David runs up the hillside. Soldiers are in pursuit. Alan Breck is hiding behind the trees)

ALAN: Duck in here, amongst the trees.

DAVID: *(Surprised)* Alan!

ALAN: Come, follow me. Quickly.

(The two friends run and escape the soldiers)

ALAN: Well, David boy, you are a Jacobite now!

SCENE TWO

DAVID: Alan Breck, you and I must part. You have killed, murdered a man.

ALAN: I had no hand in the murder. If I were going to kill a person, it would not be in my own country, to bring trouble on my Clan...even though I hate Colin Roy Campbell and all of his friends.

DAVID:	*(Wary)* Do you know the man who killed Colin?
ALAN:	*(Evasive)* Oh, David, I have a grand memory for forgetting. One thing is for sure, Colin was a Campbell and so someone will be hanged.
DAVID:	But that's not just!
ALAN:	*(Scornful)* Justice? In the Highlands? There is no justice here. There will be fifteen Campbells in the jury box and a Campbell as judge. Someone will hang for that death, you can be sure. You're a lowlander, it's different in the Highlands.
DAVID:	What shall we do?
ALAN:	Flee to the lowlands.
DAVID:	That way, I can come face to face with my uncle again. Nothing would give me greater pleasure.
ALAN:	But first, we'll go to Aucharn and meet James Stewart.
OLD DAVID:	*(Narrating)* Alan and I walked through valleys and over mountains until we reached Aucharn. We saw men carrying torches.
ALAN:	What's James doing? Has he gone mad? If we'd been redcoat soldiers, he'd be in a terrible mess. *(Alan whistles three times. James Stewart steps forward.)*
JAMES:	Alan!

ALAN:	I have a friend with me, James, a boy from the lowlands.
JAMES:	*(Sadly)* The death of Colin Campbell, the Red Fox, is a terrible thing. It'll bring trouble to us all.
ALAN:	Oh well, you take the sour with the sweet. Colin Roy is dead; let's be thankful.
JAMES:	*(Afraid)* I wish he were still alive. Who'll bear the blame for it? We will! I am sorry, I am poor company; it's the innocent that'll suffer for the death of Colin Roy Campbell.
ALAN:	King George's men will blame me, and my shoulders are broad.
JAMES:	Ah, but you are my kinsman. If they put your blame on to me, then I'll hang. *(His face turns pale)* Our friends don't want me to hang. *(Thinks)* To save myself – and the cause, I'll have to put up a reward against your friend. You do understand why, don't you? If I hang…
ALAN:	*(Quickly)* Yes, I can see the reason.
DAVID:	That's not fair!
ALAN:	*(Worried)* James, that's tough on me. I'll seem like a traitor to David.
DAVID:	We ought to put a reward against the man who shot Colin Roy Campbell, not me.
JAMES:	What, and spoil the alliance of the Clans?

ALAN: *(Looking at David)* The day will soon come when we shall drive these redcoat soldiers from Scotland. But before that, we'll make for the lowlands.

SCENE THREE

OLD DAVID: *(Narrating)* Alan and I were forced to hide from the English soldiers. We crawled along the rocks and heather while the redcoats lurked beneath them. At night we slept in caves, during the day we caught fish.

ALAN: *(Seriously)* I shall have to show you how to fight with the sword – and stay alive. Hey, somebody comes – isn't it my old friend Neil Roy? What's the problem, Neil – for I see you are a man in a hurry.

NEIL: I have looked for you two for days. I have come to warn you.

DAVID: Why? What's happened?

NEIL: James Stewart has been arrested. People believe you murdered Colin Roy Campbell, Alan. There is a bounty for your head, and yours too, David.

ALAN: Ha! I'm afraid of nobody.

NEIL: Take care. The redcoats are everywhere. There is a paper, with your descriptions written on it.

ALAN: *(Taking the paper from Neil)* Look how they have described me! *(Reading)* 'a small, pock-marked man of thirty-five or thereabouts' and you, David, ' a tall, strong lad of about eighteen; speaks like a lowlander, has no beard.'

DAVID: *(Afraid)* We can't escape the whole English army. Wouldn't it be better if we split up and met in my home town?

ALAN: Never! You wouldn't last two minutes without me.

NEIL: I had better get back to the Clan. They are upset enough that James Stewart is taken.

ALAN: *(To Neil)* Take care, Neil Roy. *(To David)* We'll head east, but not on the flat ground. The redcoats have horses, they will run us down and kill us. We'll keep to the high ground.

OLD DAVID: *(Narrating)* After walking through the night, Alan and I were very tired. Suddenly, we were attacked by a group of rugged men. They had their knives at our throats. I thought we were dead for certain. Then one of them spoke.

CLUNY: I am Cluny Macpherson, chief of the clan of Vourich.

ALAN: Ah, one of the leaders of the great rebellion, five years or so ago. I know you. We all fought together at Culloden. There is a price on your head, as there is a price on ours.

CLUNY: *(Decided)* Come, I will show you underground caves and passageways. We hide here when King George's soldiers come close to us. You can stay with us, here, if you wish.

ALAN: Thanks but I need to return to France and persuade the French to give me soldiers. I need to rescue James Stewart. He's been taken, you know!

CLUNY: I had heard. A bad business, indeed. *(Bright)* We shall walk to my cave!

(Inside the cave)

DAVID: There is a smell of cooking!

CLUNY: I like to cook. Each morning my barber shaves me. I'm like a king here. A king in exile! And I have entertained a Prince – Bonnie Prince Charlie no less. *(Laughs)* The bonny Prince was a spirited boy, but he liked his drink. Now, let's play cards before we eat.

DAVID: I am too tired.

CLUNY: No, no.

DAVID: *(Hesitant)* I cannot play cards. I never play cards.

CLUNY: *(Offended)* What in the devil's name is this? *(Draws his sword)* You are worse than King George's lot.

ALAN: *(Quickly)* The boy meant no harm. He is tired. I'm fit for a game of cards – whatever you want to play.

CLUNY: *(Angry)* Let the boy sleep! If he is rude again, I'll cut his throat.

OLD DAVID: *(Narrating)* I was woken up by Alan, nudging me.

ALAN: David, boy. I need a loan of your money.

DAVID: What for?

ALAN: Just a loan!

DAVID: Why? I don't see why.

ALAN: Do you grudge me a loan?

(David hands Alan his money and falls asleep. Later, Alan creeps over to David)

ALAN: *(Nudging David)* We must go! I've lost all our money and I owe Cluny Macpherson. He's too good with the cards.

(Cluny walks over to the friends)

CLUNY:	Have your money back! I cannot take it! I'm stuck here in a cave and I like a game of cards, but I wouldn't take the money from you two brave men.
ALAN:	And if I'd won?
CLUNY:	If you'd won, you'd have gained something. *(Grins)* Be safe!
	(He goes)
DAVID:	Cluny is a strange man.
ALAN:	We'd all end up strange, David, if we lived in these caves for too long. Cluny's lived here for almost six years!

SCENE FOUR

OLD DAVID:	*(Narrating)* I knew Alan Breck valued our friendship, but I felt I was in danger while we were together. How could I tell him we should part? I was angry that he had gambled away our money – even if Cluny had given it back! I felt humiliated.
ALAN:	David – I am sorry. I was to blame – I shouldn't play cards.
DAVID:	Yes, of course you were to blame.
ALAN:	You've not spoken to me for an hour. If you don't like my company, we can part now. I won't stay where I'm not wanted.

DAVID: *(Hurt)* I've never yet failed a friend – and I'll not begin with you.

ALAN: I owed you my life on the 'Covenant', now I owe you money, for I have none.

DAVID: *(Still wanting to quarrel)* You were stupid to play cards with that man Cluny. He gave you the money back. What have you done with the money?

ALAN: If I hadn't played cards he'd have killed you, you insulted him. *(Sheepish)* I played cards at the inn last night…and lost again.

DAVID: *(Upset)* Ha!

(They walk on in silence)

OLD DAVID: *(Narrating)* The truth was, rain had soaked us to the skin. I was ill, my head ached and I had a sore throat. We began to argue.

ALAN: *(Taunting David)* Oh, you are a lover of King George.

DAVID: *(Drawing sword)* You've fought on both sides, you told me yourself. Now you will die!

ALAN: You know I can kill you! *(Draws his sword)* But I cannot, I cannot! *(He throws his sword to the ground)*

DAVID: *(falls)* Alan – I have a fever, I am sick.

ALAN: I'll find help David – don't die! I'm sorry we have quarrelled.

OLD DAVID: *(Narrating)* We found a house. Robin Maclurren and his wife nursed me back to health. Later, we crossed by boat to the lowlands. I was not too far from claiming my inheritance.

SCENE FIVE

OLD DAVID: *(Narrating)* I arrived at Queensferry and asked for the house of Mr Rankeillor, the Lawyer.

RANKEILLOR: What a coincidence. I have just come from that house. *(Winks)* I am Mr Rankeillor.

DAVID: I am David Balfour and I have come from many strange places, but I need to talk to you in private.

RANKEILLOR: Yes, that would be best, no doubt. Come inside my house.

(He leads David into his dusty chamber, full of books and documents.)

Take a seat, Mr Balfour. If you have any business, be quick and swiftly come to the point.

DAVID: I believe I have some rights to the estate of Shaws.

(Mr Rankeillor fumbles in his desk for a paper and pen)

RANKEILLOR: Well? *(David remains silent)* Come, come, Mr Balfour, you must continue. Where were you born?

DAVID: In Essendean, in the year 1733 on the 12th of March.

OLD DAVID: *(Narrating)* I told Mr Rankeillor all about my mother and father. I told him I could prove who I was; the minister, Mr Campbell had kept all my legal documents. I also told him my uncle had had me kidnapped by Captain Hoseason.

RANKEILLOR: On the very day you were kidnapped your minister, Mr Campbell, came to see me. Your uncle told Mr Campbell that he had given you a great deal of money and you had set off for the continent of Europe. He intimated that you intended to complete your education abroad.

DAVID: *(Angry)* My uncle is a liar and -

RANKEILLOR: *(Cutting in)* Indeed, Mr Campbell told me that you intended to break from your past life. In short, he was taken in by Mr Ebenezer, although I had my doubts. I informed Mr Campbell of my doubts and we both searched for you.

DAVID: Then?

RANKEILLOR: A certain Captain Hoseason gave us a story of you being drowned.

OLD DAVID: *(Narrating)* I told Mr Rankeillor my full story. He only interrupted me once when I told him the name of my companion, Alan Breck.

RANKEILLOR: Mention no unnecessary names, Mr Balfour…above all, no names of Highlanders, that are obnoxious to the law. I am – shall we say – dull of hearing. We'll call your friend, Mr Thompson.

OLD DAVID: *(Narrating)* When my tale was told, Mr Rankeillor clapped me on the back.

RANKEILLOR: You have had a remarkable adventure, Mr Balfour. You must stay for dinner. Now, why does your uncle hate you – do you know?

DAVID: I have no idea!

RANKEILLOR: The truth is, your father and uncle loved the same woman. She had eyes only for your father. Mr Ebenezer, thinking he would gain the lady, was shocked – and aged – when he discovered the truth. A deal was done. Your father gained the lady, your uncle gained the estate. He became mean and tyrannical. As for your parents, they remained poor.

DAVID: How can my uncle's nature have changed so much?

RANKEILLOR: He came to have money, and money was all your uncle got for his bargain. His selfishness grew and grew.

DAVID: Where does that leave me?

RANKEILLOR: The estate is yours – the brothers' bargain was not legal.

DAVID: But how do I get my inheritance?

RANKEILLOR: You need to enlist your friend, er, Mr Thompson. I have a plan.

41

SCENE SIX

Alan Breck, alias Mr Thompson, hammers at Ebenezer Balfour's door. Ebenezer looks out of the top window. It is night.

EBENEZER: What's this knocking? This is not the time of night for decent folk. I'll have no dealing with night-hawks. What brings you here? I have a blunderbuss.

ALAN: Am I speaking to Mr Balfour? Have a care with that blunderbuss!

EBENEZER: *(Angry)* Who are you? What are you doing here?

ALAN: I'm here on your business.

EBENEZER: *(Shouting)* What is it?

ALAN: David.

EBENEZER: What's that? David? I'm thinking I shall let you in!

ALAN: No, I want to conduct this business on the doorstep.

EBENEZER: *(Thinking)* Well, what must be, must be!

(After a long while, Ebenezer comes to the door and unlocks the bolts. He then sits down on the steps outside his house, and holds the blunderbuss on his knees)

Now I have my blunderbuss and if you take a step nearer, you're as good as dead.

ALAN: What a polite man you are, Ebenezer Balfour!

EBENEZER: What's your business?

ALAN: I've come to talk about David Balfour. I'll let you have him for a ransom. I'm a Highlander and I captured him in Mull.

EBENEZER: *(Coughing)* He wasn't a good lad at the best of times.

ALAN: Ha – you're pretending you don't care, to make the ransom smaller.

EBENEZER: No, no. I'll not pay a ransom for a boy I hate. You can do what you want with him!

ALAN: Blood's thicker than water, you can't desert your brother's son. Well, if you don't want David, you can pay the fee for my keeping him. Either way, I want money from you!

EBENEZER: I'm not sure if I understand you!

ALAN: If you don't pay up I'll ram three feet of iron through your vitals.

EBENEZER: I have my blunderbuss!

ALAN: Power in your old hands are as the snail to the swallow. Before you pull the trigger, my sword would be through your guts.

EBENEZER: *(Afraid)* What do you want, eh?

ALAN: The lad – killed or kept?

EBENEZER: Kept, I want no bloodshed. I will not have bloodshed.

ALAN: So you'll pay a price?

EBENEZER: He's my brother's son.

ALAN: What did you pay Hoseason to kidnap the boy?

EBENEZER: Hoseason! The kidnapping's a lie. Davie was never kidnapped. He's telling you a lie.

ALAN: Strange you tell me that. Hoseason's my partner. I want the truth from you, old man.

EBENEZER: *(Sulking)* Twenty pounds. I'll pay you twenty pounds. I've paid Hoseason enough, to kidnap the boy.

RANKEILLOR: *(Stepping from the shadows)* Thank you, Mr Thompson, you have done exceedingly well. *(To Ebenezer)* Good evening, Mr Balfour.

EBENEZER: What trickery is this?

RANKEILLOR: I think, if you want to avoid jail, Mr Balfour, you will pay your nephew David two thirds of the yearly income from Shaws.

DAVID: *(Walking from the darkness and cover of the trees)* I am now a man with money!

SCENE SEVEN

The following morning. Alan and David have to say goodbye.

DAVID: Me being a lowlander and you from the Highlands, we should be bitter enemies.

ALAN: Aye, we should.

DAVID: Yet I know you for a good man.

ALAN: I shall miss you, David Balfour.

(They shake hands)

And now you will live like a gentleman.

DAVID: But first I shall continue my education. And you?

ALAN: I'll travel to France and try to raise an army to rescue James Stewart before he hangs on the gallows. One day, one day we shall win.

(He bangs his fist in the palm of his hands)

DAVID: *(Seriously)* Don't be too sure.

ALAN: *(Laughing)* We shall see, we shall see! One day, David, one day!

KIDNAPPED.

ACTIVITIES
ACT ONE: SCENE ONE.

Freeze-framing

In small groups, freeze-frame the moment when the Jacobites put their curse on King George and the traitor Campbell clan. What will their expressions look like? Will they look sorrowful, having lost a battle, or angry and determined? You decide!

Improvisation

Improvise a scene in which Neil takes the blinded Duncan McKeigh back to his wife and children. How does the family react to the news? How does Duncan feel and how will he cope, what are his thoughts now he is blinded?

Writing

Use the library to research the battle of Culloden. Then, using your research and evidence from the play, write a newspaper report of the battle for the 'Jacobite Times'. Then write another report for the 'Georgian Times', which is an English newspaper. How will the two accounts differ?

ACT ONE: SCENES TWO TO FIVE

Hot-seating

Try to remember as many facts from the play as possible. In groups of three or four, hot-seat the following characters.

Alexander - As he is dying, he is worried about David's future and the fact that he is forced to send David to Ebenezer's house.

Ebenezer - He is concerned that David may want some of the family fortune. He will be worried that he tried to kill David, but failed.

David - He is worried about the future. He will want to talk about the death of his parents and the attempt on his own life.

Writing

Write down all you can about your impressions of Ebenezer Balfour. Note his physical description, the way he moves, his voice, tone and personality. Also note his attitude towards David and what he says about his late brother.

ACT ONE, SCENES SIX TO EIGHT

Improvisation

In small groups, you are the captain and his men aboard ship. Work out the tactics you would employ to overpower and kill David and Alan.

Imagine you are Colin Roy and his men. You are collecting rent from the Highlanders. Act out a scene in which a family of Highlanders are unable to pay the rent. Their crop has failed and they are starving. What will happen? Do you strike a bargain or do you imprison or kill them?

Writing

Write the conversation that might have taken place between Captain Hoseason and Ebenezer Balfour. You will need to look at several scenes before you write this piece of dialogue. For instance, did Ebenezer intend to have David killed? How do we know this was not his intention?

Imagine David is able to write a letter to Mr Campbell from his uncle's house. In the letter he tells his father's friend all that has happened to him so far.

Dramatic moments

The sinking of the 'Covenant' is a dramatic moment in the play. In small groups, act out a different dramatic moment – perhaps an escape from an aeroplane crash, or an escape from a fire.

Research newspapers and magazines for pictures of dramatic moments, or draw the sinking of 'The Covenant'. Make a display of the class dramatic moments.

ACT TWO: SCENES ONE TO SIX.

Discussion
From all you know about James Stewart, what kind of a man is he? A generous man, a hero, a future king, a coward, a good leader? You decide, using evidence from the text. Now share your answers with the other groups and come up with a class decision.

Freeze-frame
Freeze-frame the scene where Ebenezer is trapped by Alan, David and Mr Rankeillor. Think about their expressions as Ebenezer is forced to pay David two-thirds of his family fortune.

Writing
You are David and you are keeping a diary of events, from the sinking of 'The Covenant' to the meeting of Mr Rankeillor. Write down all that happens to you, add all your thoughts and feelings.

ACT TWO: SCENE SEVEN.

Discussion
Alan Breck's Highlanders never do raise an army and Bonnie Prince Charlie dies in exile. Knowing this, do you feel the ending is appropriate? What do you think would have been a better ending to the play?

Writing
Imagine Alan Breck meets Bonnie Prince Charlie and they decide to raise an army against the English forces. What goes wrong and what happens to Alan Breck? Scriptwrite a scene or two, which might include the death of Alan.

Reflection
Compare this play with another in this series, Oliver Twist. What do the two stories have in common? Think about the hero of each, and his situation and how the stories end.